Date Due

DATE DUE

DE 09 '85	DE 1 5 '88	AG 8 '89	AP 8 '91
DE 21 '86	JA 3 '89	DE 6 '89	JA 2
NO 29 '88	FE 4 '88	DE 21 '89	DE 7 '92
JA 2 '87		JY 19 '90	DE 2 8 '92
DE 2 '87			FEB 11 '93
DE 28 '87		NO 1 '90	FEB 21 '94
JY 0 5 '88		DE 26 '90	DEC 21 '94
JY 22 '88	MR 27 '89	JA 5 '91	MAR 15 '95
APR 22 '95			MAR 06 '96
DEC 3 0 '95			DEC 17 '96 '06
MY 27 10			DEC 03 '97
JA 04 '11			DEC 23 '97
JA 02 '14			JUL 09 '98
			DEC 14 '98
			JA 17 '99
			1-7-23
	45230		Printed in USA

HOW SPIDER SAVED CHRISTMAS

BY
ROBERT KRAUS

WINDMILL BOOKS / SIMON AND SCHUSTER

NEW YORK

for Bruce, Billy and Pamela

SECOND PRINTING

SBN 671-66533-2 Trade
SBN 671-66534-0 Library
Library of Congress Catalog Card Number: 75-120904
Manufactured in the United States of America

It was Christmas Eve and I was feeling sad.

Spiders don't usually celebrate Christmas.
I don't know why. It's just a custom.

Who should I meet in the middle of my sadness
but my two friends, Ladybug and Fly.
"I want you for Christmas dinner," said Ladybug.
"And afterwards we'll go caroling," said Fly.
"You're very kind," I said, "but spiders don't
usually celebrate Christmas."

"Nonsense," said Ladybug. "See you tomorrow
bright and early."
"Bright and early," said Fly as they hurried off.
"Bright and early," I called after them.

I went home and tried to think of what I could
give Fly and Ladybug for Christmas. I knew I
couldn't go empty-handed. I had an old chair
and an old suitcase. I could give Ladybug the
old chair and Fly the old suitcase. But then
what would I sit on or pack my clothes in?

No. I must find something else to give.
I looked around my web and found two
empty boxes. I knew I couldn't give two
empty boxes. But I could put something
in them. But what?

Then in a flash I got an idea.
I filled one box with snow.

I tied it with a ribbon and wrote
To Ladybug—Joyous Yuletide. Your friend Spider.
What a nice present. And what could be more
Christmasy than snow?

But what could I give Fly? More snow? No. It
had to be something different. Then I saw some
icicles hanging from a tree. That was it! Icicles!
Another great idea!

I was very pleased with myself. Christmas was really fun.

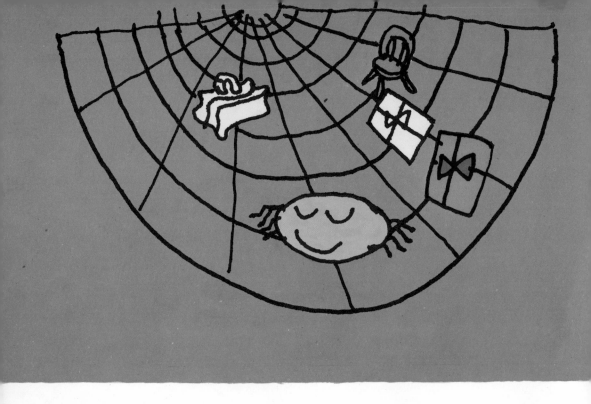

Then with my wrapped presents beside me,
I curled up and fell fast asleep.

Christmas morning shone bright and clear.
Church bells were ringing. Sleigh bells
were tinkling. I felt good as I walked to
Ladybug's house.

I peeked in the window. What a beautiful tree
Ladybug had. Fly was already there having a
cup of tea with Ladybug and stuffing himself
with cookies.
Then I remembered I didn't have to peek.
I was invited!

I knocked at the door.
"Merry Christmas," said Ladybug.
"Merry Christmas," said Fly.
"Merry Christmas," I said.

I put my two presents under the tree. "It's beautiful," I said. "Thank you," said Ladybug. "I helped decorate it," said Fly.

Ladybug handed me a pretty box. "From the
bottom of my heart and wear it in good
health," she said.

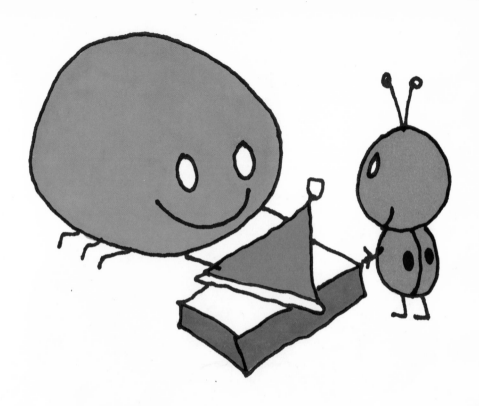

"Thank you," I said. I opened the box. It was
a wool cap.
"It will keep your head warm," said Ladybug.
"I knitted it myself."
"Thank you," I said. "I've always wanted a
warm head."

"From me to you," said Fly.
"Thanks, Fly," I said.

I opened the box. Inside was a snapshot of Fly
in flight.
"It will remind you of me," said Fly.
"Thank you," I said. "Next to a warm head, I've
always wanted to be reminded of you."

Ladybug gave Fly a warm wool scarf.
"I'd sooner had a cap," grumbled Fly.

Fly gave Ladybug a snapshot of himself in flight. It was just like the snapshot he gave me.

"Thank you," said Ladybug. "It will remind me of you."

"That's right," said Fly.

"Now open my presents," I said.
"They seem to be leaking," said Ladybug.
"Leaking is right," said Fly. "It's a flood!"

They opened their presents anyway.
"Water!" said Fly.
"Mine too," said Ladybug. "But be polite."
"Thanks for the water, Spider," said Fly. "It's just what I wanted."
"Yes, thank you," said Ladybug. "Water has so many uses."

"You're very welcome," I said. I was all choked
up and I began to cry. My eyes began to smart
and burn as if I were in a smoky room. Great
Scott! I *was* in a smoky room!

"Ladybug! Ladybug!" I shouted. "Your house
is on fire!"

"It's the stove!" cried Ladybug. "My cupcakes will burn!"

"Let's all run for our lives!" screamed Fly.
"No, wait," I said, calmly grabbing a box of
water. "Do as I do."

"Heave Ho!" I said.
"Heave Ho!" said Fly.
"My poor cupcakes,"
sighed Ladybug.

The fire was put out in no time, but nothing remained of my presents for Fly and Ladybug but puddles on the floor and two soggy boxes. "Gee," I said, "I can't tell you how sorry I am that your Christmas presents got thrown on the fire."

"Water he calls Christmas presents," muttered Fly.

"Shhh," said Ladybug.

"What I mean is," said Fly, "your Christmas presents put out the fire and saved the day!"

"Yes, Spider," said Ladybug, kissing me on the cheek. "You saved the day. You saved Christmas!"
Well, I guess in a way I did. And I was very happy I did, because it turned out to be a very merry Christmas for us all.

THE END